W9-ARY-159

15793 EN
Tale of Benjamin Bunny, The

Potter, Beatrix
ATOS BL 4.4   ATOS 2000: 681
Points: 0.5

THE CHILD'S WORLD®

The Tale of Benjamin Bunny

Written by Beatrix Potter • Illustrated by Wendy Rasmussen

Published in the United States of America by The Child's World®
1980 Lookout Drive • Mankato, MN 56003-1705
800-599-READ • www.childsworld.com

ACKNOWLEDGMENTS
The Child's World®: Mary Berendes, Publishing Director
Editorial Directions, Inc.: E. Russell Primm, Editor; Dina Rubin, Proofreader
The Design Lab: Kathleen Petelinsek, Design; Victoria Stanley, Production Assistant

LIBRARY OF CONGRESS CATALOGING-IN-PUBLICATION DATA
Potter, Beatrix, 1866–1943.
  The tale of Benjamin Bunny / by Beatrix Potter ; illustrated by Wendy Rasmussen.
    p. cm. — (Classic tales)
  Summary: Peter's mischievous cousin, Benjamin Bunny, persuades him to go back
to Mr. McGregor's garden to retrieve the clothes he lost there.
  ISBN 978-1-60253-292-2 (library bound : alk. paper)
  [1. Rabbits—Fiction.] I. Rasmussen, Wendy, 1952– ill. II. Title. III. Series.
  PZ7.P85Tak 2009
  [E]—dc22   2009001629

The Tale of Benjamin Bunny

ne morning a little rabbit sat on a bank.

He pricked his ears and listened to the *trit-trot, trit-trot* of a pony.

A carriage was coming along the road. It was driven by Mr. McGregor, and beside him sat Mrs. McGregor in her best bonnet.

As soon as they had passed, little
Benjamin Bunny slid down into the
road and set off—with a hop, skip, and
a jump—to call upon his relations, who
lived in the wood at the back of Mr.
McGregor's garden.

That wood was full of rabbit holes. And in the neatest, sandiest hole of all lived Benjamin's aunt and his cousins: Flopsy, Mopsy, Cotton-tail, and Peter.

Old Mrs. Rabbit was a widow. She earned her living by knitting rabbit-wool mittens and fingerless arm warmers. (I once bought a pair at a bazaar). She also sold herbs, rosemary tea, and rabbit tobacco (which is what we call lavender).

Little Benjamin did not very much want to see his aunt.

He came around the back of the fir tree and nearly tumbled upon the top of his cousin Peter.

Peter was sitting by himself. He looked poorly and was dressed in a red cotton pocket handkerchief.

"Peter," said little Benjamin, in a whisper, "who has got your clothes?"

Peter replied, "The scarecrow in Mr. McGregor's garden." And he described how he had been chased about the garden and had dropped his shoes and coat.

Little Benjamin sat down beside his cousin and assured him that Mr. McGregor had gone out in a carriage, and Mrs. McGregor also, and certainly for the day, because she was wearing her best bonnet.

Peter said he hoped that it would rain.
At this point, old Mrs. Rabbit's voice
was heard inside the rabbit hole, calling,
"Cotton-tail! Cotton-tail! Fetch some
more chamomile!"

Peter said he thought he might feel better if he went for a walk.

They went away hand in hand and got upon the flat top of the wall at the bottom of the wood. From here, they looked down into Mr. McGregor's garden. Peter's coat and shoes were plainly to be seen upon the scarecrow, topped with an old wool cap of Mr. McGregor's.

Little Benjamin said, "It spoils people's clothes to squeeze under a gate. The proper way to get in is to climb down a pear tree."

Peter fell down headfirst. But it was of no consequence, as the bed below was newly raked and quite soft.

It had been sown with lettuces.

They left a great many odd little footmarks all over the bed, especially little Benjamin, who was wearing clogs.

Little Benjamin said that the first thing to be done was to get back Peter's clothes, in order that they might be able to use the pocket handkerchief.

They took them off the scarecrow.
There had been rain during the night.
There was water in the shoes, and the
coat was somewhat shrunk.

Benjamin tried on the wool cap, but
it was too big for him.

Then he suggested that they should
fill the pocket handkerchief with onions,
as a little present for his aunt.

Peter did not seem to be enjoying
himself. He kept hearing noises.

Benjamin, on the contrary, was
perfectly at home and ate a lettuce
leaf. He said that he was in the habit
of coming to the garden with his father

to get lettuces for their Sunday dinner.

(The name of little Benjamin's papa was old Mr. Benjamin Bunny.)

The lettuces certainly were very fine.

Peter did not eat anything. He said he should like to go home. Presently, he dropped half the onions.

Little Benjamin said that it was not possible to get back up the pear tree with a load of vegetables. He led the way boldly toward the other end of the garden. They went along a little walk on planks, under a sunny, redbrick wall.

The mice sat on their doorsteps cracking cherrystones; they winked at

Peter Rabbit and little Benjamin Bunny.

Presently, Peter let the pocket handkerchief go again.

They got among flowerpots, frames, and tubs. Peter heard noises worse than ever. His eyes were as big as lollipops!

He was a step or two in front of his cousin when he suddenly stopped.

This is what those little rabbits saw round that corner!

Little Benjamin took one look, and then, in half a minute less than no time, he hid himself and Peter and the onions underneath a large basket.

The cat got up and stretched herself—
and came and sniffed at the basket.

Perhaps she liked the smell of onions!

Anyway, she sat down upon the top
of the basket.

She sat there for five hours.

I cannot draw you a picture of Peter
and Benjamin underneath the basket,
because it was quite dark, and because
the smell of onions was fearful. It made
Peter Rabbit and little Benjamin cry.

The sun got round behind the wood,
and it was quite late in the afternoon.
But still the cat sat upon the basket.

At length there was a *pitter-patter,*
pitter-patter, and some bits of mortar fell
from the wall above.

The cat looked up and saw old Mr.
Benjamin Bunny prancing along the top
of the wall of the upper terrace.

He was smoking a pipe of rabbit
tobacco and had a little switch in his hand.

He was looking for his son.

Old Mr. Bunny had no opinion whatever of cats.

He took a tremendous jump off the top of the wall onto the top of the cat, cuffed it off the basket, and kicked it into the greenhouse, scratching off a handful of fur.

The cat was too much surprised to scratch back.

When old Mr. Bunny had driven the cat into the greenhouse, he locked the door.

Then he came back to the basket and took out his son Benjamin by the ears and whipped him with the little switch.

Then he took out his nephew Peter.

Then he took out the handkerchief of onions and marched out of the garden.

When Mr. McGregor returned about half an hour later, he observed several things that perplexed him.

It looked as though some person had been walking all over the garden in a pair of clogs—only the footmarks were too ridiculously little!

Also, he could not understand how the cat could have managed to shut herself up *inside* the greenhouse, locking the door upon the *outside*.

When Peter got home, his mother
forgave him, because she was so glad
to see that he had found his shoes and
coat. Cotton-tail and Peter folded up
the pocket handkerchief, and old Mrs.
Rabbit strung up the onions and hung
them from the kitchen ceiling, with the
bunches of herbs and the rabbit tobacco.

ABOUT BEATRIX POTTER

When Beatrix Potter (1866–1943) was growing up in England, she did not go to a regular school. Instead, she stayed at home and was educated by a governess. Beatrix didn't have many playmates, other than her brother, but she had numerous pets, including birds, mice, lizards, and snakes. She enjoyed drawing her pets, and they later served as inspiration for her books.

As a young girl, Beatrix enjoyed going for walks in the country. She began drawing the animals and plants she saw. For several years, she also kept a secret journal, written in her own special code. The journal's code was not understood until after Beatrix died.

In 1893, when Potter was twenty-seven years old, she wrote a story for a little boy who was sick. That story became *The Tale of Peter Rabbit*. In 1902, the book was published and featured illustrations drawn by Potter herself. Her next book was *The Tale of Squirrel Nutkin*, which was published in 1903. Potter went on to write twenty-three books, all that were easy for children to read.

When Potter was in her forties, she bought a place called Hill Top Farm in England. She began breeding sheep and became a respected farmer. She was concerned about the farmland and preserving natural places. When she died, Potter left all of her property, about 4,000 acres (1,600 hectares), to England's National Trust. This land is now part of the Lake District National Park. Today, the National Trust manages the Beatrix Potter Gallery, which displays her original book illustrations.

ABOUT WENDY RASMUSSEN

Drawing from the time she could hold her first crayon, Wendy Rasmussen grew up on a farm in southern New Jersey surrounded by the animals and things that often appear in her work. Rasmussen studied both biology and art in college. Today she illustrates children's books, as well as medical and natural-science books.

Today, Rasmussen lives in Bucks County, Pennsylvania, with her black Labrador Caley and her cat Josephine. When not in her studio, Rasmussen can usually be found somewhere in the garden or kayaking on the Delaware River.

OTHER WORKS BY BEATRIX POTTER

The Tale of Peter Rabbit (1902)

The Tale of Squirrel Nutkin (1903)

The Tailor of Gloucester (1903)

The Tale of Benjamin Bunny (1904)

The Tale of Two Bad Mice (1904)

The Tale of Mrs. Tiggy-Winkle (1905)

The Tale of the Pie and the Patty-Pan (1905)

The Tale of Mr. Jeremy Fisher (1906)

The Story of a Fierce Bad Rabbit (1906)

The Story of Miss Moppet (1906)

The Tale of Tom Kitten (1907)

The Tale of Jemima Puddle-Duck (1908)

The Tale of Samuel Whiskers or, The Roly-Poly Pudding (1908)

The Tale of the Flopsy Bunnies (1909)

The Tale of Ginger and Pickles (1909)

The Tale of Mrs. Tittlemouse (1910)

The Tale of Timmy Tiptoes (1911)

The Tale of Mr. Tod (1912)

The Tale of Pigling Bland (1913)

Appley Dapply's Nursery Rhymes (1917)

The Tale of Johnny Town-Mouse (1918)